Agua

Water Was More than a Friend

LUCKY SUNDAY .O.

INK START MEDIA
265 Eastchester Dr Ste 133 #102
High Point NC 27262

Agua: Water Was More than a Friend

Lucky Sunday

The Journey with Agua

Years ago! In the Eastern part., I was born and brought up in the sea quarter; 1 GREGO and my family lived at the beach side with one of the American families whose names were Cool and his wife, Kate. They were our family friends and we were the only people in that neighborhood at the beach side until summer before other people will come from different elements of the world to the beach and every summer, we do have an enormous event.

Cool and Kate had one child named AGUA meaning "water", who was my only friend because he was the only son of his parent's and I GREGO was also the only son of my parents. AGUA and I played, stayed and did things together and AGUA are year older than me and every summer, both of us would play together at the beach and I know what pleases AGUA and he knew what I want and likes. We were more than friends if there is any word, also were more than a brothers. AGUA and I preferred food like barbecue and Greek native wine and our hobbies would do beach—dance and we dance for people to watch at the beach every summer.

Then AGUA and I were like endless brothers not just friends, at the age of nineteen we planned and talking how we could be rich in life. We both really want to be famous because we were doing well in our studies in school and we don't want to end up as beach performer boys. So! We agreed that after the following summer we would travel to the U S.

So, the summer came. One day, at 1pm in the beach after AQUA and I had finished dancing while my father and AGUA's Dad were roosting barbecue my mum and AGUA mum were sitting down beside them. I and AGUA were at the water swimming and there were batch of people in the beach that every day both of us came out from the water to eat some from the roosted lamb. We wanted to go back to the water. Then, Aqua's mum called us back. She gave them presents such as hand Chains and they were very contented.

So! Both went to the water as they were in the water. I GREGO felt some stingy movement within him and GREGO said to AGUA to get out of the water. All of a sudden, a mermaid came out very close to us. We could not move on or swim out, for about ten minutes as other people were running out of the water and she was looking profound to us and she was so gorgeous. All I could see where she and other three sexy attractive girls. I was heavy as if I am going weak from their chest above the waist down were skin of fish. Then I saw AGUA diminishing into the water with his eyes closed. Then, I screamed "hay, AGUA No!!!" Then something lifted me up and landed me to the water and before I landed, I couldn't see AGUA, none the women again, they both disappeared on water, then they rushed me out of the water so the safety team put me into the ambulance to the hospital before the ambulance get to the hospital, I was awaked and I was very physically strong. When the ambulance got their doctor and they were trying to work on me, then I dragged them like a mad-man and I ran out I saw the ambulance car at the entrance of the door. I took the ambulance and I crowd it rapidity back to the beach, before I get there? All the police and rescue teams had come to the beach searching for my friend, my only brother. I tried to go into the water to look for him with them the police held me and I was lamenting and very cheerless. Hum! So, on the day 2 of searching, some of the American diver's team came because AGUA was an American citizen. Three weeks after AGUA was no were to be found by any, two days before this happened both of us was wishing and talking that we wish we could be wealthy and still be good friends a brother together in life; I said to AGUA that "let it be this form", then AGUA answered "how?" I said to him, "no matter what comes between us, we should take to each other our favorite food when we bring our favorite to one another? And we shall come together as friends and brother again." AGUA and I agreed strongly to this and wrote the paper and kept it into the Bible, because of the painful feeling I couldn't remember all that we said to each other.

Few days after, AGUA mum and Dad were moving their belongings out of the house to travel to the states. When I saw them, I ran to meet them to ask them "what? And where they are going to?"

AGUA mum said to me that she is living the pain to a place. When I twist back, I saw my parent stuffing out also, then I ran into AGUA house to his room I found his passport on the floor I picked it and I hid it then I came out of the house. My Dad said to me, "let us go." And I answered to him "no" that I will come with AGUA; Then they all left me over there, later in the evening I went to my grand mama house in the city I were living with her and going to my college from there I cannot talk to anyone on my college except one beautiful, an American girl who was a hip pop dancer winner in my college, I found it difficult to floor with other people.

One day, I went back to our former house at the seaside to pass a time out there. Getting to my room I saw my picture and AGUA own unknowing to me that KYSS, my college friend went to look and ask after me in my grand mama's house and my gram mum tell her to check on me at the seaside.

Then I saw the paper that we wrote, as I was reading it all the dance I and AGUA where dancing was blinking on my memory then I had a voice calling my name and it was KYSS. She was looking for me and she banged into the house then I kept the paper to myself.

Then we left together (This was three year and four months after) every night & day I do think and dream about AGUA and the paper that I saw was with me, one day I went to KYSS to teach me how to dance because she dances hip pop and I dance native beach dance. She thought me a new step it was a bit difficult for me to learn. I was going to her until I leaned some new step of dance from KYSS, I was preparing to go and dance alone in the seaside for AGUA. So, I went to the church to pray as I was coming back from the church a man with a white Greek came to me from nowhere and gave me a bottle of Greek wine and he said give it to your friend, swiftly he disappeared.

When I got home, I was thinking and I went out to give the wine to KYSS because she is the only friend that I have since AGUA left. As I got to KYSS house I was told that KYSS has left to the US for a dancing confront with her team in the states.

Then I went back home and told my gram mum that I will be coming home in three-day time and she tried to stop me but she could not. Then I left to the house in the beach said with some of my stuff and the first day I came out of the house with our old radio that we used to play together and I put it on and started crying then. After a few I started dancing all day nothing happened till dark then I went inside the house, the next day I started dancing and danced suddenly I saw an object started moving in the water and the reflection was like a large mirror to my eye's for about 6 minutes. I wanted to stop dancing and I stopped the music after a while I couldn't see anything with my eyes. I fell down and started crying then I fell asleep down on the ground there.

The next day, I woke up and I saw myself lying inside the house and inside our house was now a very hygienic beautiful woman. Then I saw that old man who gave me wine and he put beside me an old box that looked like a treasure box of one fit high and five centimeter long he called the box Calabash, and inside the box was a roasted rabbit. I was very hungry that I could not refuse to accept. I started eating the meat, and the flavor was like of the normal lamb meat for me. Then he gave me Greek native wine in the bottle and said to me give this to your brother then I asked him, "who are you and who is my brother?" Then he gave me a copy of that article that AGUA and I wrote then, I quickly drag off my shoe I brought out my copy from where I kept it below my foot inside the shoe I was surprised and a kind of frightened I looked at the man and the old man nodded his head with a slide of smile, and said to me in your brother kingdom this wine gives them ecstasy & it tranquillize their powers then he left as a vast glow of light.

Then I went out close to the water where I was dancing before with the wine by my side with the music song then I started dancing with the music for seven hours. I was going weaker than I recalled the step KYSS thought me, now I started the steps, few minutes after I saw the sea coming to me in a gigantic shape with speed I were still dancing then I started calling his name "AGUA! "AGUA!!! Speedily, big, big fishes started jumping up to the water, up to the water.

Then after I couldn't see any fish and everywhere was cold and still with springs falling as if it was raining, I took the wine and I opened it and I drank from it and called AGUA name and said, "This is your wine come and have it." When I said that, I saw the water moving as if someone is coming out then. I saw a very giant man with a long hair handsome look getting to the waist. He stops and he shucked his head and the water slashed on me and there was an extraordinary might in that water, as the water torched me, he pushed me back from where I was standing to about fifty miles long distance and fell on the ground. Then I wanted to run away then he called my name to come back then I twisted and said to him, "If you're my friend my brother AGUA you should come to me because I called you first." I knew he was AGUA but I wanted to be convinced because he was so very gigantic more than a human being size. He wanted to refuse then I started reminding him the way we use to dance then he stops and said to me give me that wine and I answered him I called you first come and I will give you.

I was terrified because he was so big and handsome. He came out close to the sand I saw him, and he was AGUA my friend, my brother. Then I walked close to him from his waist down was skin of fish then I slashed the wine to his body then he screamed and there was a vibration everywhere in that place even same of the houses in the city who were built with glass was affected and some were cracked and some were broken to pieces because of his extraordinary powers. The wind was blowing. I stood still, I was much braved and after a while he changed to normal human bin size but the fish part was still there. Hmmm! he appeared as beautiful young women me why, he was a gentleman with long green hair and brightness skin, this was like a trance but it was real and it happened to me.

Now, he was rolling on the ground and I added more wine on his body then I ran back, few hours later the fish part disappeared but he couldn't get up from the ground because his legs were so little that he was unable to stand. Then I wanted to go and help him up, then the old man came and called my name and I turned the old man said, "Come inside the house" and I went. When I get there, he put on my neck a local made necklace and I asked him, "what this? "And he said to me that, this is a cavalry. He told me that so long I live with AGUA that the cavalry tree most is on my neck and with it there shall be kwon any arm or evil against me, then the old man left as a glow again.

Then AGUA was to come inside with naked body when I saw him and I ran to take a cloth to cover him and helped him. Then I quietly put on the fire so that the house will be hot for he was very cold and he couldn't say a word to me I try to everything for him to talk he didn't say any word, So I started dancing and he started smiling.

The next day, someone came to rang the bell and I went to open the door and it was the policemen and they told me to live the house that the house is in a restituted area and I said," ok" to them. I went back inside again the bell range and when I got there, I saw the old man my aid again and he said to me that I should make food with the wine that AGUA will eat from the food and he start talking as before and he will remember as we were before also told me that he now had extra power to do some impossible things.

 When I got inside, I started making some food and he was crying I feet for him and when I finish making the food, I gave him and he started eating and he sinuses and water purl out from the top and everywhere were full with water and he started telling me that the food is nice and he asked me that are we not going to school today? And I answered him that we are dancing today, and then we danced.

After then we both went to the city in my gram mama house; many people were looking at him because AGUA is now more handsome with his long black hair; after some days I called my gram mum to loan me some money and she said alright unknown to me that my gram mum was not having sufficient cash with her, so she went to her friend telling her that I want to travel to that U S, and her friend refuses her; then AGUA had it because of his strength power when you're talking about him, he do hear it except me because of what is in my neck, and he said to me that we are traveling to the state I didn't tell him then I answered him I wanted to surprised him; he said alright and he went out and called me to come with him and he pick up two gravel on the grand then we went back inside the house and he cut a little from his hair with the stones in the serving dish and he gave me a knife to cut him I was wondering and I sprite away the knife and I ask if he is crazing? After adequate disagree then I took the knife and cut him then the water that came out of his eyes he kept it in another plate and he asked me to torch the water with my finger and I did he said I should put the water to where I cut with knife and I did the same, I said what? No, and he said with a laud voice do it!!! I shacked. then when I put it, the cut was hailed rapidly; AGUA added the pieces of the hair and the stone together in one plate with the water that came out of is eyes, before my two eyes the two stones changed to valid diamond, he gave me one that I should have my and asked me what do you want that he don't have? I was silent and he said is only life that is impossible for men to give but others? He smiles a bit.

Then I ran out with my diamond stone and he try to stop me he couldn't, I went to the shop to check it and it was real then I sold it for 21 thousand drachmas and I ran to the church to pay my fixed to GOD before I went home. AGUA was very mad at me! But later he said to me that I did good thing and I answered him what? He said, for giving to God his own that was very nice.

The next day, both of us with my gram mum went out for shopping, the customer was scaring at us and they were wondering the way we were spending cash all the people were looking at AGUA height and handsomeness' no one new whom AGUA was, so one of the customer service called the policemen unknowing to me but AGUA new it because of his stringy power, so when the policemen came; AGUA make the wind start blowing and the policemen started laughing AGUA was rolling his leg as a cycle on the grand and before we left AGUA smile at the customer service ladies and sinuses in the shop and water came from nowhere then we go with our goods. a day after I went to the US embassy for visas after three the visa was given to me and I told AGAU that we have to travel to the U S, because your passport is with me and he said that he knew, and I was like quiet for second, and I said yeah, yeah. After your parent left, I went to your old house and I found AGUA passport it was with me since and he smile and said No! I asked why? He

asked me do you want me to go with you. I said yes, then he said, go and get an aquarium if you wish to go to US with me, I say to him I didn't get it, he said go get it. Then I went to the street market it took me some hours to get a good-looking aquarium made with glass and I brought it home getting home he said to me that I should listing to him for all he wants to say is that he needs my help and I became curious, I answered help? He said yes. I asked how? Then he starts explaining to me the reason why he asked me to go get an aquarium, he said that he will be going with the aquarium and I asked how? He said that if he wants to go on hero plain that the flight can't take it all, and the plain would not be able to carry water that my name is AGUA it means water, as he measured water, huge water slashed out of the top of the room and all over my bodies were felled with water and he smile at I was about to get annoyed I were still standing in front of him then he blow he with his maw in a twinkle of an eyes my body and the water on the flow dry up, then he said shall we? I said Oh! Sure…;

Then AGUA asked me to filled the aquarium with water I was wondering but not afraid, after filling it he said to me that I should put it in the room and he will be looked in that room alone, and he said you should not come in to the room until the time you wish to go to the airport then you can come in and you shall fine the aquarium and you will take it with you and I said what about you? And he looked at me and smile with slow-motion he every say any word and he walk across me where I stood to the room and he shut the door. Then I walked to my room and rest on the bed but I was not comfy, and I get off from the bed I went direct to where I kept the old Calabash box and when I opened the box, I saw a piece of paper which was writing in Greek language (Για να τον δείτε όταν φτάσετε στον προορισμό σας πηγαίνει στο μπάνιο και σπάει το ενυδρείο).

It means; to see him when you get to your destination goes to the bathroom and breaks the aquarium. Immediately I read the piece of paper in my hand what was writing on it faded out from the paper in shocked and drop it back to the box.

So! When it was time for me to go airport, I walk to his room door and I opened it slowly and I couldn't see AGUA in the room all I saw was the aquarium with fish inside and I wanted to go back from the room I couldn't move back and the door shut itself, if I try to step back the door will shut then I move forward close to the aquarium and pick it up and the door opened then I understand that he was the fish inside the aquarium; now my thought was how will I take the aquarium with me into the flight? Then, I brought out one luggage and one other side bag on my shudder with aquarium on my hand before I got to the front gate I saw a man who dress like the chief of navy officer with one old rich English car, I was standing in front of his face, the man can't talk he only move his mouth and I couldn't understand I also tried to read his lips still I couldn't, he knew and all I could see was the man were using his hand to write on air like (me voy al aeropuerto vengo déjame caer). I was able to see and red what he wrote on air because it was in Latin language and then I said oh! I speak Spanish too, what he wrote means; I am going to the airport come let me drop you, and I asked him what is your name? In Spanish (¿cuál es su nombre) and He wrote it again with Latin saying LIBRE it means FREE and I walk close to the man and the door of the car opened, inside the care were so model like a million-honour hum!!! And Mr. Ayudar gets to the driver seat and inside the car was cover with smock before a minute; I saw myself and Mr. Ayudar at the airport. Then Mr. Ayudar took the aquarium from me and I followed him and he was just going and going all the security was just showing him a sign of force salutation I was just walking with him smiling nodding my head with slow motion at the security that is how I got into the flight and I looked at my passport when I sat down it was stamped, then I turned to look at Mr. Ayudar I didn't see him and the aquarium was on top of the seat beside me and I quickly pick up the aquarium and cover it with my jacket then I put it into one of the luggage hole above my seat; other passengers started coming inside the flight, when I turned to my lift I saw Mr. Ayudar standing at the last exit door, then I tried to walk down to him other passengers was an obstacle on the footpath then I strangled and pushed some passengers down and also I fell down too when I rise up my head I saw him going to the restroom and I gets up from the flow quickly and rushed to the toilet door and knock saying Mr. Ayudar, Mr. Ayudar no one answered, I opened the toilet door and entered Mr. Ayudar was not in and all I saw was the pallid Navy clothes that he was wearing at the floor I screamed like a real African man Eh! Eh! Eh! With my two hands on my head I closed the toilet door rapidly and I was in there for about ten or more minutes having many, many thought like to just leave everything in the air flight and jump out and go start a new life because I thought that I got a new friend not knowing that Mr. Ayudar is just going to left me with his Navy uniform; now I remembered that the aquarium was not too save living it up there the crew or others can see it and it will get me into other trouble then I quickly pick up the clothes and rushed back to my seat I couldn't sleep all other passenger were sleeping except one fat and big young boy whom may be around the age of seventeen he was seating across the footpath on the other row, he was looking trying to know what was going on with and any time I looked at him our eyes will meet each other in a direct contact and I will smile a funny smelly as if I don't have problem to tackle.

So; when we arrived at the airport I quickly take my bag and the aquarium which I covered with my jacket as I was coming out of the flight entrance a lady came took the aquarium from my hand hollow and said follow me, I stood still I thought that I have gone into trouble with the American immigration, she turned back said again come with me, then I start walking with her and talking when I asked her what is your name she said that is not necessary, that she came to give me a hand because she saw that my luggage and the hand bag were too much for me and was not too sure of all she were saying then she asked me my passport and I was so depress that it look like I want to really use the toilet this is the way I can explain it; then I put my hand at my trouser pocket and gave her my passport and she walked me across the security to the passport inspector she gave them my they look at it and gave it back to them when she gets to the arriving hall she gave me my passport and the aquarium and she walked away, although the aquarium were covered with my jacket and to me she didn't know what was inside the jacket even the shaped was like of a cube and a4 size up till now I don't know who she was and I never see her again in my life…

The lady walks away to the same direction where we came out from, so! I quickly rushed to the toilet with my bags and the aquarium; as I was rushing into the restroom getting there I saw that fat young boy coming out from the toilet mistakenly he hit me with his shudder the jacket and the aquarium fell on the floor and the aquarium were broken to pieces the fish that was inside were jumping on the floor and the fat boy was still there with me and fish stop jumping and he started growing big and bigger to the size of human then he started changing to human and the fat boy said oh my GOD, and he wanted to run out then I dragged him and the both of us fell on the floor fighting then water pump out from no were and I let the fat boy go.

So, the fat boy didn't know how the fish turned to become AGUA and walk to the side where the fish was and I saw him he was AGUA without clothes on his body then I got the bag and covered him with one of my wooding jackets and I brought out the Navy cloth that Mr. Ayudar left for him to put on before the fat boy came back with the people. He went to call; we walked out of the airport. I could see them from outside as the people were running to the toilet side getting there, they couldn't find anything and the fat boy saw me from afar then I waved my hand to him and we departed from the airport….

When we got to the city, AGUA didn't want to go to his parent house. I understood because they we never believed it and also AGUA is not like before now have a different handsomeness look and other powers with him. And we went to one of the lodges with the money that left with me; that night as we were sleeping, I feel that the room was very cold. Then I woke up and I found out that the room floor was filled with water, so I woke him up and it was ten in the morning and I took out our soft that I could carry with me and we both moved out we were walking in the avenue Conner all the bad guys were looking at us. Then the diamond that was with AGUA cut down on close to the bad boys and he went to picked it up; then the guys came and said to him give us that stuff, is that stone and some said is that diamond but AGUA never answer them and he was still standing at the same spot, I try to talk with the guys but AGUA said to me shut up!!! I couldn't stop then one of the boys punch me and I

fell on the grand then AGUA came to me and help me and said to me that I should move out of the location and I said no;

Then AGUA shouted at me with a slight of smile and I said, "alright" and he is now annoyed because the guys torched me and when he got angry he would be smiling, I am the only person who can stop him; and he move closed to the bad guys, he put the diamond stone on the grand and said to them come and have it and all the boys were coming and they were about seven of them, they started trying to get him but none of them couldn't torch the diamond non torching him, if they try to punch him it will look like they are hitting a slashed of water, the water will stop their hand in other not to get AGUA, and AGUA was using his hair to slash them water. And the water came out form his hair and there is power in that water, I was looking at them from afar and AGUA suspended two of the boys in the air and froze four with ice the remaining one was on the grand tight with AGUA long hair and the other bad boys saw it and they ran away. Then I cried with a thunderous voice and called his name AGUA please stop and I stoned him with a coin that was with me, then he stops and those boys were free and those who were suspended fell from up to the grand and I move close to him and his body and his clothes were very new and dried up as if nothing happened and we left.

So we went back to the lodge and we are spending many day now then I was mad because the hotel management told me that our money will be expired 2am in the morning, that night I left my hotel room for casino house to watch and I asked one man to help me with some money, $20 the man asked the security to trolled me out and they did, so I went back to the hotel room and when I entered the room everywhere in the room was quiet and I try to open AGUA's room I couldn't, then I knocked on the door and called his name and he came through my back and answer me here I am then I turned and he said to me open; I did and the door opened, what I saw is money the room was filled up with money and he asked me what do I want? I was shot of words as we were talking at each other the hotel manager knocked at the door then I took some money

from the one in AGUA room and give the manager, then I took some money and ran out to buy luggage's and I came back to the room and started leading the money in and I said to AGUA let go out because it was already 1pm day time and we went out.

When we got to one of the biggest shopping center unknown to me that AGUA has set his eyes on one gorgeous girl and I didn't know that they knew each other I thought that the girl was falling for AGUA handsomeness and his height because that is what the women went, and he walk close to the beautiful Queen than I move into the shop and AGUA diamond felled down and the girl go down with a sign of respect as if she is greeting a traditional person and she picked up the diamond for him and they started talking as a friend I was sparing them and I was so very glad atlas he talk to other person because he don't use to talk to other people except me, so he came to me and we went forded walking and we were still in the shopping center when I had someone calling my name and turned back it was KYSS my old friend in the college who thought me a new dancing step, she ran to me and hug me so I was about to introduce her to AGUA he said to me that he knew KYSS and I understood then I talk over it; so we went to the restaurant KYSS, AGUA and I as we were there KYSS and I was eating food and AGUA was only taking wine because I took one bottle along with me and I always take it along whenever we are going out, so some wine purl on AGUA' s clothes then KYSS went to the waiter before she came back to her sit with us the white clothes was new as if nothing happened.

Since AGUA came back from the water world, he always dresses with white clothes so we all left and KYSS left us and when we got home, I was bordering because if the police found out about the money he may not be in trouble because I knew he is not just a human he has other powers with him but, what about me? I sit down I never say a word because I was thinking of what to do, then AGUA called me and said to me let us go and play game in casino house and I answered him and said no!!! What? How are we going to spend all this money? I talk and talked then he said to me that when we get there that I will found the way out about how we are going to squander the money, so we went and there was a group of people, bad men in the house playing game and the price in the game was too big that they said that anyone who win the game will be the owner of the casino house.

Then AGUA told me that the bad men with tattoos all over their bodies are using magic power to play the game also with the Asia men are using remote of the machine which is the key to wine because they knew how the machine were made and he said, with that no one can wine it and I say to him so let us get out of the casino house, then He said to me that I should go and join them to play and I answered him no and I went out and I was going then he came to me and said to me that if I play the game that the solution of the money in the house is there that if only I will play, so I decided and we went back then I started playing, I play and played every one was losing and drawing the game and each time anyone loses or draw all the money will go to the casino house. I went to the game house with one big traveling bag wheat of $1m, now I was left with $6 thousand and I turned back and I looked at him where he was sitting down and I was very angry at him then he came and site with me and gave me some money and he torch with his saliva unknown to other people I wanted to asked why but he turned his back at me then I started playing, the first one I play I draw the game and AGUA said to me play more I did because I has no chooses and there are enough money that I was even looking for how we will spend it without the police coming to ask how did we get all the money.

By now, AGUA came close to me and he held my hand and he started smiling abruptly the place was cold and I played the game and I was having the highest number then I won it all!!!

Then, the other Don and their boy started fighting us and there was a commotion in the building, and AGUA use is power and I was also fighting before the policemen came down AGUA and I was sitting as if nothing happened. So, the press came and after that there was a red carpet and funs and our dream to become famous life came to pass, but throughout all this AGUA never say a word to any of the press; after then he said to that I should go and bring all the money that was in the hotel, now I can spend money without looking back, so we move to a new big hose of our own.

Then AGUA said to me that our purpose is to help the poor and some people that are in need and with what we have that we can make a little impart to others people life; Then we started going from a place to place, first we established our own aid organization and we went to the prostituted that use to stay at the road in the night to work and we invite them after that we went to the street and some of the communities we invite them and many people came and the bad guys that AGUA dead with when we first came to the country was there too, we start by giving jobs and we open businesses for those that went to have their own business and some went back to school. And we stop a lot of things with money in that state that we were many of the red-light houses close because we buy it and pay them off and every one that work in there and the hopeless were now having home.

So! When the parent of AGUA saw us on the TV and they called my parent on the phone they never believe what they saw, so my parent travel down to the country and each family was looking for us.

This is where the problem come from one of a world model were running after AGUA to be for her not knowing that this will curse anger to the kingdom of water because AGUA has already married to the manmade. So they went to afflict that girl with fattiness she weren't able to be coming to AGUA because she were now on medication and to all the girls who were trying to have AGUA the manmade will appear to them and afflict them with fattiness, It was hard for me to live AGUA to be alone because KYSS was now my girlfriend; A one day came that AGUA said he went to go for date with that beautiful girl that he meet at the shopping center, KYSS and I was at home;

Then I plan a supra birthday for AGUA and it was a very large gathering the don and many of the Americans star & celebrity was in the party, there I engage my girl KYSS and that beautiful girl AGUA went for date with, whom he meets at the shopping center also came to the party with other six beautiful sexy girls, when I saw them and I knew that they are from water because their beauty was more then

what I do see and I can see whom they are and AGUA was sitting with them drinking Fanta together with them,

They all knew me but they can't do me any harm me because of what was on my neck.

So! some men want to asked two of the girls who were sitting with AGUA to come and dance and they refuses then AGUA told them to go and dance with the men, any other people can't see what they are and all people can see is the beauty but now in the party I was seeing them well from their waist down was fish and they are not genuine human but people seeing that they are walking, and unknown to me that my girl KYSS went to AGUA where he was sitting down with those girls to ask him dance and the QUEEN was angry for that as my girl were talking one of the girls hit KYSS on her shudder and my girl flow away to the war and she fell, then I ran to KYSS as I was helping her up the thing that old man put on my neck droop down so the two girl that was dancing sinuses and water came out from nowhere people was shouting eh!!! And happy because they thought it was path of the party, then I went and told AGUA to calm them down and the beautiful girl who was the QUEEN and she smack me and I was sliding on the grand then all the girl started fighting me with their powers and AGUA were trying to support me and to stop them and the water was increasing and we were still fighting and people were running away from the party hall there was a perplexity until I saw were my necklace is then I quickly put it back to my neck and all the girl disappeared and the party was closed then KYSS was rushed to the hospital, as I was in the hospital with KYSS alone I sat down and the old man torch me on the sudden and I shocked and he started telling me that they came from the water to take AGUA back because they didn't want AGUA to get marry to human being apart from their realm that is the reason why they came but he don't want to go with them, so they are angry and want to use force,

Then I asked him what will I do for him to stay? And the old man was silent for a minute and answered to me and said that he will dead! that is when all will be end and if they take him away all the money and everything will go with him, and the old man gave me one little bottle of oil he said to me that if I see that there is danger or risk I should use some of the oil to torch AGUA and the oil is very powerful it the oil of God and they can't take him and he will die; The old man talk about life and said; The ways of life is that, it's not the viewer who counts; not the man who points out how is the strong man stumbles, or where the doer of actions could have done them better. The praise belongs to the man who is actually in the ground, whose face is blemished by dust and sweat and blood; who strives valiantly; who comes short again and again, because there is no effort without error, conflict before victory; but who does actually strive to do the actions; who knows great enthusiasms, the great devotions; who spends himself in a worthy cause; who at the best knows in the end the triumph of high achievement, and who at the worst, if he fails, at least fails while daring greatly, so that his place shall never be with those cold and timid souls who neither know victory nor overcome.

I agree and the old man torched my front head and he torch KYSS as well and he said; this life is what you make it. No matter what, you're going to mess up sometimes, it's a universal truth. But the good part is you get to decide how you're going to mess it up. Many will be your friends—they'll act like it anyway. But just remember, some come, some go. The ones that stay with you through everything—they're your true best friends. Don't let go of them. Also remember, sister makes the best friends in the world but this is an endless brother. As for lovers, well, they'll come and go too. And baby, I hate to say it, most of them—actually pretty much all of them are going to break your heart, hmmm AGUA depart from me when the dream finally comes true Oh!!! But I couldn't give up because if I give up, I'll never find my life cover. I'll never find that half who makes me whole and that goes for everything, but many people think that is only when one is your own blood that matters no! This is a friend more than a brother. Just because you fail once, doesn't mean you're going to fail at everything. Keep trying, hold on, and always, always, always believe in yourself, because if you don't, then who will, sweetie? So, keep your head high, keep your chin up, and most importantly, keep smiling, because life's a beautiful thing and there's so much to smile about, and he move away as a glow of light and KYSS was hailed and we left.

Then when I got home AGUA called me and told me that he so sorry for what happened and he said to me that there will be a beach party coming up that I should make it larger than any other party in town, then I knew what is going to happen and I prepared my best so that they can't take him, as we were talking that day? Our parent located us and we were very excited and AGUA started talking to everyone who was there and I was not surprised because I knew what was going on that his time on earth is up and he was excited with all, KYSS was having a bit understanding of what is going on and by now AGUA was more handsome, so my girl KYSS came to me and asked me what is going on and I took her out of the place and I tell her a little of how everything started, AGUA father were dead by now his only her mum that came with my parent to look for us, AGUA mum was not alright with the transformation look of AGUA body and his hair, I knew it and I told my girl KYSS to be convincing AGUA mum with another conversation; A day before the party day AGUA buy her mum a big house and a new car, her mum was not still convinces.

The party day came that I make everyone to put on white clothes, and it was 2pm as we were at the beach for the party seven girls came out of the water and they put on white clothing and everybody was looking at them, AGUA and I were talking and the girls went to deferent, deferent place to sit down.

Then AGUA and I were still talking and AGUA said to me that he wishes if he came modify the ways of life; that money can't do all things, and I knew what he was saying but I answered him why? And AGUA said to me, that is only on this earth that money can really speak but he can't stop death;

Then AGUA said to me, can you help him? Because two is better than one, and I reply him saying, with GOD on my side I will, KYSS my girl saw those girls that came out of the sea she came to meet I and AGUA, and she said to us lest live this place and AGUA answered her, we can run but we can't run out of the earth and he can't hide on earth because 70% of the earth is covered by water.

I gave my heart to the mountains the minute I stood beside this sea with its spray in my face and watched it thunder into foam, smooth to green glass over sunken rocks, shatter to foam again.

I was fascinated by how it sped by and yet was always there; its growl shook both the earth and me; Water is also one of the elements on earth, during the incident of my life I never know that there's another world inside this earth that we can't see with our own ordinary eyes without been spiritual until the end of all I memorize that the most beautiful of God's creations; It is both wet and cold, heavy, and with a tendency to descend, and flows with great readiness.

It is the Holy Scripture has in view when it says, and the darkness was upon the face of the deep.

And the Spirit of God moved upon the face of the waters.

Water, then, is the most beautiful element and rich in usefulness, and purifies from all filth, and not only from the filth of the body but from that of the soul, if it should have received the grace of the Spirit. These I say that there is much living in the water then the dry land of which you can't see.

There's thrilling about the sea which people don't know about and they will be draw to it, many want to love by it, want to swim in it, look at it and play in it. It was a living thing that as unpredictable as a great stage artist. It could be calm and welcome, opening its arms to embrace its audience one moment, but then could blow up with its stormy tempers, flinging people around, wanting them out, attacking coastlines and breaking down islands.

In the sea are the violence and terrors of which psych has warned us but if you ride these monsters deeper down, there in the sea is just like the way we are in dry land that we see some area in our communities that some zoon are violent and while some are nice people, so; that is why you see during the summer people die in the water at the beach, they are a lot of things you can't see with your eyes, I wish you could eye it with your natural eyes now! Imagine this that you're walking along the street and all of a sudden, all the houses are not to be seen with your eyes and you were able to walk any part me why the owners can see you but you can't see them with your natural eyes due to you are just human and you didn't notice that you are stepping on someone dining table full of meal, wedding cake or stepping on someone head while he/she is sleeping and you feel that you are swimming so tell me how you think that the person will act/react you??? If you drop with them father over the world's rim, you fine what our sciences cannot locate or name, the substrate, the sea or matrix or the heavens which buoys the rest, which gives goodness its power for good, and evil its power for evil the united field, our complex and mysterious caring for each other, and for our life together here.

This that I said, it is not to shock any but to discover out. It had a friendly side too, as it enjoyed the crowd, tossed the children about, occasionally gave sailors helping hands; all this are done with a secret. The ride with my friend AGUA makes me to know little about the sea and the dry land.

I wish I could describe the feeling of being at sea, the anguish, frustration and fear, the beauty that accompanies threatening spectacle, the spiritual communion with creatures in whose domain I sail.

There is a magnificent intensity in life that comes when we are not in control but are only reacting,

Living, surviving; my own cosmology is convoluted and not in line with any particular church or philosophy. But for me, to go to sea is to glimpse the face of God. At sea I am reminded of my insignificance of all men's insignificance. It is a wonderful feeling to be so humbled.

Oh! It amazed how the excitement come upon me to tell it all in the expedition of writing, the heart can speed up with anticipation as it does, really, throughout the chase itself of whales. I can vow it, I will tell you even if other writers may not. My heart is beating fast:

I was in pursuit: I want my victory and you should see and heard and above all feel the reality behind these words; For they are real but is cover, is not like a mask that I would have to strike through as simple appearance, or inferior, deceitful appearance; the words need not to be that type of mask, but the mask such as the wonders of the early men, a cover that expresses rather than conceals the inner felling.

Those girls that came out of water stood up from where they was and one of them walk to were the table of food and drinks were kept and turned them down because they were looking for trouble and who will make them go more angry, then the people try to stop her and the commotion started; AGUA took some sand from the grand and put it on my girl KYSS pocket and said because no one can move the grand so nothing can aim you KYSS; and it look like the people were overcoming the girls in the fight so they started using there evil powers one of the girls were fighting the three of us KYSS, AGUA and I; so those girls ran close to the water and banded there head on the ground and suddenly the wind started blowing evilly everyone started running away there were still a lot of people so the QUEEN of those girl come out of the water, all we could see was from her chest up she was every big like an image, and she was at the same position and she started calling AGUA and the wind were still blowing, she was very beautiful giant woman and people were running away, the chain that I use to handcuff AGUA with myself got cut and AGUA walking close to the water to meet them so my girl KYSS ran to him and cut his back with bottle and AGUA stop walking and one of the girls point her hand to my girl KYSS and my girl flow about fifty miter and stood but nothing hurt her then I ran to KYSS and AGUA started walking to meet them.

Then I picked out the little bottle which the old man gave to me and when they saw me coming to meet AGUA, the girls started blowing me back with the wind from their mount. Then I strong on through the wind and torched AGUA with the oil. When I torched him with the oil, and the reaction force pushed me to scattered the chairs and the table that was built for the party and AGUA also fell on the grand, and I unconscious for about 30 minute after, I wake up I fine my way out and the woman entered into the water before I fell on the grand, and the policeman were already there but the power was more then what they can stop; they saw everything that happened, the woman left by changing into gigantic fishes and the police wanted to start shutting and I was shouting no! Stop!!! And they all stop and the fishes were all departed and the ambulance came and we rushed AGUA to the hospital; when we got there AGUA smile and said to me that AGUA WAS MORE THEN A FRIEND; that he want to live, after saying that about four doctors came in one of them was the boss the doctor came to confirm him and they said AGUA is dead and I could see his belly started changing to fish and all the doctor ran away only one doctor stood and I could see something like a glow in human form before I knew he disappear the rest bodies totally change to a big fish.

unknown to me that the real human of AGUA is sating at home with the Old man and the body that is lay on the bed was the fish spirit in him; after the incident that happened in the hospital I went to my house when I got home, all I could see was two men seating and they backing me I could not see their face and they were charting I wanted to run at AGUA called me to come back and I turned and the old man said to me he is the one then I looked it was AGUA and he is now like a real human size and if the same age with me; then I hit him I can see that he felt the ache because before you can't hit him even if you dose he is going to feel any hurt and I still not convinces I quickly rushed to get water and pour it on him and then I knew it was real and we hug each other… ! Then the old man said that the valley must takes all that comes is way without choices then AGUA asked him give more understanding about what you said? Then, the old man said the secrete has just began and I asked why? The old man said that the spirit is mute and in 14 days and he left as a glow of light…

Let all seat back and watch after fourteen days of the journey with AGUA!

Water Was More Than A Friend
The Journey With Agua

9 781961 254336